VIRTUAL VIPERS

Unmasking the Secrets Behind Online Financial Scams

RK THE
NAWAB

AF658310

BlueRose ONE.com
Stories Matter
NewDelhi • London

BLUEROSE PUBLISHERS
India | U.K.

Copyright © RK The Nawab 2024

All rights reserved by author. No part of this publication may be reproduced, stored in a retrieval system or transmitted in any form or by any means, electronic, mechanical, photocopying, recording or otherwise, without the prior permission of the author. Although every precaution has been taken to verify the accuracy of the information contained herein, the publisher assume no responsibility for any errors or omissions. No liability is assumed for damages that may result from the use of information contained within.

BlueRose Publishers takes no responsibility for any damages, losses, or liabilities that may arise from the use or misuse of the information, products, or services provided in this publication.

BlueRose ONE.com
Stories Matter
NewDelhi • London

For permissions requests or inquiries regarding this publication, please contact:

BLUEROSE PUBLISHERS
www.BlueRoseONE.com
info@bluerosepublishers.com
+91 8882 898 898
+4407342408967

ISBN: 978-93-6261-179-6

Cover design: Tahira
Typesetting: Tanya Raj Upadhyay

First Edition: July 2024

Radhey Radhey

"THERE ARE NO GET RICH QUICK SCHEMES"

One word of advice for scammers from Garud Purana

सारमेयादन: धन लूटने वाले, भ्रष्टाचारियों को नर्क में विचित्रप्राणी काट-काट कर खाते हैं।तामिस्र: जो व्यक्ति दूसरों के धन, स्त्री और पुत्र/बेटी का अपहरण करता है, उस दुरात्मा को तामिस्र नाम की यातना सहनी होती है। इसमें यमदूत उसेअनेक कष्ट देते हैं

I don't know whether this is true or not but if its 1% is true than its going to hard..all scammer in this world be aware

Rest IPC will get you one day..

Dedicated to everyone who lost their hard earned money to these SCAMMERS hope you recovered your money and get helped from police..

DATA ON ONLINE SCAMS…

According to a report of business standard

Now India has been in top ten countries who are facing cybercrime along with Russia and china.The number of financial frauds in India, including those reported for ATMs, grew 65 per cent in 2022 as compared to 2021, and double in 2023 , the Finance Ministry has told the Parliamentary Committee, as reported by The Hindu BusinessLine (BL). The amount involved in these frauds has, moreover, nearly doubled.

"In 2021, we saw the total frauds reported for ATMs and other frauds were about 1.08 million and the value was Rs 1,119 crore. That means for every 67,000 transactions, one fraud was committed. For 2022, 1.78 million is the number we have. The amount Hamburge

Home / Economy / News / Financial frauds in India rose 65% between 2021 and 2022: Finance Ministry

Financial frauds in India rose 65% between 2021 and 2022 and now its double in 2023: Finance Ministry

National Payment Corporation of India informed the Parliamentary Committee that, on average 10,000 customers are impacted by cyber frauds in India every month

The number of financial frauds in India, including those reported for ATMs, grew 65 per cent in 2022 as compared to 2021, the Finance Ministry has told the Parliamentary Committee, as reported by The Hindu BusinessLine (BL). The amount involved in these frauds has, moreover, nearly doubled.

"In 2021, we saw the total frauds reported for ATMs and other frauds were about 1.08 million and the value was Rs 1,119 crore. That means for every 67,000 transactions, one fraud was committed. For 2022, 1.78 million is the number we have. The amount is Rs 2,113 crore. For every 64,000 transactions, one fraud was committed," the ministry was quoted as saying in the BL report.

The ministry also listed four trends in cybercrimes in the country. These are" use of crypto for money laundering and terror financing; use of mule accounts with fake addresses, use of international online betting sites for money laundering and terror financing, and use of lending apps and apps for investment.

Separately, the National Payment Corporation of India (NPCI) informed the committee that, on average, 2,000 customers are impacted by cyber fraud in India every month. Also Read: UPI-related scams account for 55% of total digital payments frauds in India

DGCA-like body recommended

The Parliamentary Committee, according to BL, has, in return, recommended the establishment of a centralised regulatory authority for cyber security on the lines of the Directorate General of Civil Aviation. The main aim of the body will be to "shoulder the responsibility of safeguarding the nation's critical IT infrastructure and networks from cyber threats".t is Rs 2,113 crore. For every 64,000 transactions, one fraud was committed," the ministry was quoted as saying in the BL report.

Another report on livemint tells that

A total of 9,053 cases of frauds were reported in various banking operations amounting to ₹45,598 core in 2021-22, shows the RBI data on trends and progress of banking in India, shows the latest RBI data on trends and progress of banking in India.

Year	Total value of frauds (₹crore)
2011-12	4,497
2015-16	18,491
2019-20	1,66,576
2020-21	1,18,417
2021-22	45,598

The I4C, established by the Ministry of Home Affairs, serves as a framework for law enforcement agencies to combat cybercrime. The significant escalation in reported cases is evident from 2019 to 2024, with 26,049 complaints recorded in 2019, 257,777 in 2020, 452,414 in 2021, 966,790 in 2022, 1,556,218 in 2023, and 740,957 in the first four months of 2024 alone.

Most victims fell prey to online investment fraud, gaming apps, algorithm manipulations, illegal lending apps, sextortion, and OTP scams. In 2023, the I4C reported over 100,000 investment fraud incidents. Digital arrests resulted in a loss of Rs 120 crore across 4,599 cases in the initial four months of 2024. Trading scams accounted for 20,043 cases, leading to a loss of Rs 1,420 crore to cybercriminals during the same period.

source RBI /Business Standard/ livemint

TABLE OF CONTENTS

INTRODUCTION

In the big complicated world of the internet, there resides unseen threats that can strike when you least expect it. Welcome to the chilling reality of online financial scams, a shadowy underworld ruled by cunning con artists and ruthless fraudsters. They slither in the digital landscape, poised to strike with venomous intent. These are the virtual vipers.

"Virtual Vipers" takes you on a heart-stopping exploration of this sinister realm. It is a book that uncovers the darkest corners of the internet, revealing the intricate tactics employed by online scammers to defraud innocent victims of their hard-earned money. It is a world where trust is exploited, and vulnerability is a lucrative business.

This book is not just about recounting tales of deceit and manipulation. It is a guide, a beacon of light designed to help you navigate the murky waters of online financial scams. It aims to arm you with the knowledge and tools needed to identify these threats and shield yourself from their deadly bite.

The internet can be a treacherous terrain, but it doesn't have to be. With the right knowledge, you can protect yourself and your financial assets from these virtual vipers. This book will expose their tactics, reveal their methods, and guide you on how to stay safe in the digital age.

As you delve into these pages, prepare to be intrigued, shocked, and enlightened. Brace yourself for an eye-opening expedition into the dark recesses of the online world, where every click can lead to a potential trap. Remember, knowledge is power, and in this digital battlefield, it is your strongest weapon.

"Virtual Vipers" is more than a book; it is a survival guide for the digital age. It will open your eyes to the grim reality of online financial scams and empower you to safeguard your digital presence. So, get ready for a thrilling dive into the dark depths of online financial scams. The virtual vipers are waiting, but with this book in hand, you will be ready to face them.

CHAPTER 1: RAJEEV'S RUIN

Rajeev's Internet Lure

The web has turned into a playground for the innocent and the evil in this age of fast internet and advanced technology. The story starts with Rajeev, an ordinary teen who is good at technical things. Like many teenagers at his age, he is fascinated by this virtual world and its numerous possibilities. Little did he know, he was about to fall prey to a dangerous trap in what might have seemed an innocuous place.

Rajeev was very bright in computer programming and coding taught to him by his elder sister . He went further than mere gaming or social media but also explored the internet expanses. However, this curiosity would soon bring him into unexpected peril.

One day while on the internet surfing, Rajeev saw an ad on a coding competition. It had a mouth-watering cash prize as well as an opportunity to be employed by one of the best technological companies in the world. For Rajeev it was just too fine to let go of that chance. He clicked on it and landed on a professional-looking website which is well-organized. His instincts did not warn him of any danger; thus, he immediately signed up for the contest using his real name.

Weeks flew by with every day seeing him receive continuous updates from those who organized the competition.His instincts did not alert him to any danger, and he promptly registered for the competition by providing his personal information.

Days turned into weeks, and Rajeev received regular updates from the competition organizers. He was engrossed in preparing for the competition, dedicating all his free time to perfecting his coding skills. He was so absorbed in his preparations that he did not notice the subtle signs of danger looming on the horizon.

Suddenly, one day, he found himself logged out of his email account. He tried to recover his account, but all his attempts were in vain. He was perplexed and clueless about what had happened. As he delved deeper into the issue, he realized that his email account had been hacked.

In the following days, Rajeev began to notice other strange occurrences. His social media accounts were compromised, and his computer started behaving erratically. He was devastated when he discovered that his bank account had been emptied. The gravity of the situation dawned upon him when he realized that he had become a victim of an online scam. The coding competition was a trap set up by cybercriminals or "virtual vipers "to gather personal information and exploit unsuspecting individuals like him.

Rajeev's story serves as a stark reminder of the traps of the virtual world. It underscores the importance of internet safety and the need to be vigilant while sharing personal information online. The world of the internet is not always as it seems. It is a world where the line between reality and illusion is blurred. It is a world that is as dangerous as it is fascinating. Rajeev's experience is a cautionary tale for all internet users, a reminder that one must tread carefully in the virtual world.

In the urge for justice Rajeev once again dive into this web scam and try to figure out what actually happened.He filled a complaint against virtual scammers under cybercrime and become vigilant about any other suspicious activities on internet trying to contact other victims. He started searching for a person who can help him or guide him to recover his money and data.well his search for truth will lead him to worthy man later on we see.

CHAPTER 2: MOHIT'S MISFORTUNE

The Deceptive Deal

Mohit, a hardworking architect residing in the shining city of Gurgaon, was known for his attention to detail in both his professional and personal life. With a loving wife and two young children, every decision he made was with their well-being in mind. It was this very devotion that made him a prime target for the cunning tactics of online fraudsters.

One fateful day, while browsing the internet for investment opportunities to secure his family's future, Mohit stumbled upon an enticing offer promising high returns in a short period. The scheme, disguised as a legitimate investment opportunity, boasted of guaranteed profits through a complex web of investments in various industries.

Intrigued by the prospect of financial stability for his loved ones, Mohit decided to take the plunge. He invested a substantial portion of his hard-earned savings into the scheme, convinced by the persuasive promises of the fraudsters.

Initially, everything seemed to be going according to plan. Mohit received regular updates on his investment's purported growth, further fueling his optimism. However, as time went on, cracks began to appear in the facade of the scheme.

When Mohit attempted to withdraw a portion of his earnings to cover an unexpected expense, he was met with excuses and delays from the fraudsters. Alarmed,he dig deeper into the workings of the scheme, only to uncover a tangled mess of deceit and manipulation.

It became apparent that the promised returns were nothing more than smoke and mirrors, with new investors' funds being used to pay off earlier investors in a classic Ponzi scheme fashion. Mohit realized with a sinking feeling that he had fallen victim to a sophisticated financial fraud, one that had robbed him of his life's savings and shattered his trust.

Refusing to succumb to despair, Mohit embarked on a quest for justice. Armed with evidence gathered through countless hours of research and documentation, he filed a complaint with the authorities and cybercrime, determined to hold the fraudsters accountable for their crimes.

Months of legal battle was going on and his was dealing with high stress and future of his secure family was also suffering , for the sake of justice Mohit started to seek help and desperately want to solve his financial crunch.

Ultimately, Mohit understand that there is no get rich quick scheme everything is a deceit. It teaches us to remain vigilant, to question the allure of quick riches. He became more vigilant and consious and joined online community for awareness against cybercrime.

CHAPTER 3: RIYA'S REGRET

Riya had always been driven by a passion for journalism, a fire that burned brightly within her since childhood. Growing up in the bustling city of Mumbai, she dreamed of making a name for herself in the world of media. Little did she know that her aspirations would lead her down a treacherous path of deceit and betrayal.

One ordinary day, while scrolling through her social media feed, Riya came across a tantalizing advertisement promising the job opportunity of a lifetime - a prestigious position as a senior journalist in a renowned media company based in New York City. The offer seemed too good to be true, with an attractive salary package and the chance to work in the heart of the media industry.

Excited by the prospect of fulfilling her dreams, Riya wasted no time in applying for the position. To her surprise and delight, she received a prompt response inviting her for an interview via video call. The interview went smoothly, with Riya impressing the HR representative with her skills and experience.

However, her joy soon turned to skepticism when the HR representative mentioned that in order to secure the job, Riya would need to upgrade her skills through an exclusive online course offered by the company. Assured that this additional training would set her apart from other candidates and enhance her chances of success, Riya hesitated but ultimately agreed to enroll in the course.

Despite the hefty price tag attached to the course, Riya's eagerness to pursue her dreams outweighed her doubts. With her eyes set on the promised salary and the allure of a prestigious position in New York, she reluctantly paid the exorbitant fee and began her training.

Weeks passed, and Riya diligently completed the online course, pouring her heart and soul into mastering the skills required for her dream job. However, as the promised date of her joining approached, she grew increasingly anxious when no offer letter arrived.

Desperate for answers, Riya reached out to the HR representative, only to be met with vague excuses and stalling tactics. It was then that she realized the harsh truth - she had fallen victim to a carefully orchestrated scam.Heartbroken and betrayed, Riya found herself grappling with the devastating realization that her dreams had been shattered by greed and deception. The once-promising job offer had turned out to be nothing more than a cruel hoax, leaving her with a bitter taste of betrayal.

There was a little difference in the domain name of real company and the scammers they use small L in place of capital "i" and victim Riya didn't recognise the scammers website is not that genuine one.

But Riya refused to let this setback define her. Drawing strength from her resilience and determination, she vowed to use her experience to expose the truth behind the scam and prevent others from falling victim to similar schemes.

Armed with her journalistic instincts and unwavering resolve, Riya delved deep into the dirty world of online fraud, tirelessly gathering evidence and unraveling the intricate web of deceit.

Though the journey had been fraught with challenges and setbacks, Riya emerged victorious in her quest for justice. Her courage and tenacity not only brought closure to her own ordeal but also served as a beacon of hope for countless others who had fallen victim to similar schemes.

As Riya stood before the world, a symbol of resilience and integrity, she knew that though her dreams may have been temporarily derailed, her spirit remained unbroken. With a energy of solving this scam she filled a complain to cybercrime branch and waited for scammer get exposed.

CHAPTER 4: RAVI'S REPERCUSSIONS

The False Promise

In the bustling city of Mumbai, Ravi, a dedicated social worker, poured his heart and soul into running his NGO for five long years. His noble efforts were fueled by a genuine desire to uplift the community and make a positive impact on society. Little did he know that his altruistic endeavors would lead him into the clutches of a cunning villain, Balbir Singh Mann.

Ravi's NGO had been sustained by the generous donations of friends and colleagues, and he had managed to keep it afloat through his sheer determination and passion for social change. However, his world was turned upside down when he stumbled upon a government project aimed at raising awareness in the community.

Excited by the opportunity to expand his organization's reach, Ravi successfully completed the project, only to find himself ensnared in a web of corruption and deceit. The government grant came with a hefty bribe demand of Rs. 10lac leaving Ravi feeling uneasy but ultimately compliant in hopes of future collaborations.

It was during this vulnerable moment that Balbir Singh, a notorious figure in the NGO community, made his nefarious entrance into Ravi's life. Under the guise of friendship and partnership, Balbir Singh lured Ravi into a sinister trap, promising him access to lucrative government projects worth millions.

Balbir Singh, with his smooth talk and charming demeanor, painted a picture of success and prosperity,enticing. Little did Ravi know that behind Balbir Singh's facade lurked a ruthless and cunning scammer, preying on the innocence and goodwill of honest social workers like himself.

Their initial interactions were cordial, with Balbir Singh offering Ravi seemingly opportunities to collaborate on government projects. As their relationship grew, Balbir Singh began to slowly manipulate Ravi into investing his life savings into securing these projects.

At first, Balbir Singh suggested that Ravi contribute a modest amount towards securing the projects, assuring him that it was a necessary step to insurance of getting these government projects by hand. However, as time went on, the demands grew more insidious, with Balbir Singh pressuring Ravi to invest larger and larger sums of money.

Blinded by the promise of making a difference in the world, Ravi reluctantly complied, unaware of the true extent of Balbir Singh's deception. With each transaction, Balbir Singh's hold over Ravi tightened, until he found himself completely at the mercy of the cunning scammer.

Their conversations were filled with false promises and deceitful assurances, as Balbir Singh continued to exploit Ravi's trust for his own gain. Despite growing suspicions, Ravi remained hopeful that his contribution would pay off, convinced that he was contributing to a noble cause.

But as the truth began to unravel, Ravi found himself trapped in a web of lies and deceit spun by Balbir Singh.The promised government projects never materialized, and Ravi's life savings were drained away by the cruel villain who had preyed upon his trust and goodwill.The all government websites and projects suddenly disappeared from internet and Ravi realised that Balbir Singh a strongly connected Man in world of NGOs will never returned his money on the other hand he will make his NGO blacklist and will also prove that Ravi has given bribe to government officials for grants and projects,it was devastating and and big setback for Ravi image.

Desperate and betrayed, Ravi realized too late that he had fallen victim to a professional scammer who had cunningly disguised himself as a friend and ally. Balbir Singh's true nature as a heartless villain was revealed as he callously looted Ravi of everything he held dear – his trust, his integrity, and his hard-earned money.

As Ravi stood amidst the wreckage of his shattered dreams, he vowed to expose Balbir Singh for the villainous fraudster that he was. With unwavering determination, he embarked on a mission to bring justice to all those who had fallen victim to Balbir Singh's deceitful schemes.

Though the road ahead would be long and fraught with challenges, Ravi refused to back down. For he knew that the bitter truth of NGOs scams must be brought to light, and the villainous Balbir Singh must be held accountable for his crimes against humanity.

Ravi though was fearful of his NGO goodwill filled complaint against Balbir Singh Mann and his CA under fraud and cybercrime.Hopelessly waiting for justice Ravi joined a nation wide community for NGOs and start awaring about these online scams done to NGOs.

CHAPTER 5: JYOTI'S JEOPARDY

The Digital Deception

Jyoti, a young woman with a thirst for adventure, found herself drawn to an enticing advertisement promising a luxury vacation package. The prospect of escaping the monotony of her daily routine was irresistible, and she eagerly clicked on the ad, her heart racing with excitement.

As she read through the details of the offer, her eyes widened with anticipation. A luxurious getaway to a tropical paradise, complete with five-star accommodations and exotic excursions - it was a dream come true. All she had to do was provide her credit card information to cover the nominal "processing fees."

Fueled by the allure of the promised vacation, Jyoti hastily entered her credit card details and clicked "submit," her mind already drifting to sandy beaches and azure waters. But as the seconds ticked by, a sinking feeling began to gnaw at her stomach.

Days turned into weeks, and Jyoti's anticipation turned to anxiety as she waited for confirmation of her booking. But instead of receiving a confirmation email, she was met with silence. Confusion turned to dread as she realized that something was terribly wrong.

Frantically checking her credit card statement, Jyoti's worst fears were confirmed - her card had been maxed out, drained of every last penny by unknown charges. The luxury vacation she had dreamed of was nothing but a distant fantasy, replaced by the harsh reality of financial ruin.

Feeling helpless and betrayed, Jyoti reached out to her bank for assistance, only to be met with indifference and bureaucratic red tape. With nowhere else to turn, she sought solace in online forums, hoping to find others who had fallen victim to similar scams.

But the online world offered little comfort, as Jyoti found herself inundated with stories of others who had been similarly deceived. Desperation clawed at her heart as she realized that she had been just one of countless victims of clickbait scams, preyed upon by faceless predators lurking in the depths of cyberspace.

With her savings depleted and her trust shattered, Jyoti found herself at a loss for what to do next. The world seemed to close in around her, suffocating her with a sense of helplessness and despair. Where could she turn for help when even the authorities seemed powerless to stop the relentless tide of online fraud?

As she sat alone in her darkened apartment, Jyoti vowed to never again fall victim to the siren song of clickbait advertisements. Though her dreams had been dashed and her faith shaken, she refused to let the scammers win. With a steely resolve, she began the arduous journey of rebuilding her life, one small step at a time, determined to emerge stronger and wiser from the ordeal.

As the reality of her situation sunk in, Jyoti felt a sense of betrayal wash over her. She had fallen for the enticing promises of a luxury vacation, only to be left with nothing but a mountain of debt and a shattered sense of trust.

Desperate for answers, Jyoti turned to the internet in search of guidance. Hours were spent scouring forums and reading articles, hoping to find a glimmer of hope.amidst the sea of despair. But each click only seemed to lead her deeper into a labyrinth of scams and deceit.

With no clear path forward, Jyoti felt a sense of isolation creeping in. She hesitated to confide in friends or family, ashamed of her gullibility and fearful of their judgment. After all, how could she explain that she had been swindled out of her hard-earned money by a simple click of a button?

The days turned into weeks, and Jyoti found herself consumed by a sense of hopelessness. The weight of her financial burden grew heavier with each passing moment, threatening to crush her spirit beneath its suffocating grip.

In a last-ditch effort to seek justice, Jyoti mustered the courage to file a complaint with the authorities. But as she navigated the maze of bureaucracy and paperwork, she couldn't shake the sinking feeling that her cries for help were falling on deaf ears.

As the weeks stretched into months, Jyoti began to resign herself to her fate. The scammers remained at large, their identities shrouded in anonymity as they continued to prey upon unsuspecting victims with impunity.

But amidst the despair, a flicker of determination ignited within Jyoti's heart. She refused to be defined by her circumstances, to allow the actions of others to dictate her future. With a newfound resolve, she vowed to turn her pain into purpose, to become a voice for those who had been silenced by the cruel machinations of online scammers.

Armed with her experiences and fueled by her passion for justice, Jyoti embarked on a mission to raise awareness about the dangers of clickbait scams. Through advocacy and education, she sought to empower others to protect themselves from falling victim to the same fate that had befallen her.

Though the road ahead would be fraught with challenges, Jyoti faced it with courage and conviction. For she knew that even in the darkest of times, there is always a glimmer of hope - a light that shines brightest in the face of adversity. And with each step forward, she moved closer to reclaiming her life and finding the redemption she so desperately sought.As Jyoti delved deeper into her quest for justice, she discovered a community of fellow victims who shared her pain and frustration. Together, they formed a support network, offering each other solace and solidarity in their shared struggle against online fraud.

Driven by a sense of purpose, Jyoti became an advocate for change, using her voice to shine a light on the dark underbelly of the internet. She shared her story far and wide, speaking at conferences and media outlets, urging others to remain vigilant and wary of the dangers lurking behind every click.

But as she fought tirelessly to raise awareness, Jyoti couldn't shake the gnawing feeling of injustice that plagued her every waking moment. The scammers who had robbed her of her peace of mind continued to evade accountability, their identities shrouded in secrecy as they continued to prey upon unsuspecting victims.

Determined to hold the perpetrators accountable, Jyoti refused to back down. She collaborated with law enforcement agencies and cybercrime units, providing them with valuable insights and evidence to aid in their investigations.

Months passed, and Jyoti's efforts began to bear fruit. With the help of her advocacy and the tireless dedication of law enforcement, several key figures behind the clickbait scam were apprehended and brought to justice.

Though the road to recovery was long and arduous, Jyoti found solace in knowing that her actions had made a difference. Through her perseverance and determination, she had reclaimed her sense of agency and emerged stronger and more resilient than ever before.

As she reflected on her journey, Jyoti realized that while she may have been a victim of online fraud, she was also a survivor - a testament to the indomitable human spirit and the power of resilience in the face of adversity.

Armed with the knowledge that she had made a tangible impact in the fight against online scams, Jyoti looked towards the future with renewed hope and optimism. Though scars from her ordeal may linger, she knew that she would never again allow herself to be victimized by the deceitful allure of clickbait scams. Instead, she would continue to stand as a beacon of strength and resilience, inspiring others to do the same. Jyoti filled a complaint on cybercrime and waiting for justice.

CHAPTER 6: KIRAN'S CALAMITY

The Fraudulent Scheme

Kiran and Techy, two adventurous souls, delved headfirst into the world of cryptocurrency and Web3 gaming with dreams of striking it rich in the burgeoning digital economy. Excited by the promise of financial freedom and the thrill of cutting-edge technology, they eagerly poured their hard-earned savings into the crypto market, eager to ride the wave of innovation.Kiran and Techy's journey into the world of cryptocurrency and Web3 gaming began with excitement and optimism. They meticulously researched various projects, attending online seminars, reading whitepapers, and scouring forums for insights. After countless hours of deliberation, they finally decided to invest their hard-earned savings into a portfolio of promising meme coins and speculative tokens.

Their initial investments yielded promising returns, fueling their confidence and igniting their appetite for more. Encouraged by their early success, Kiran and Techy began to invest more aggressively, pouring larger sums of money into the market in pursuit of even greater gains.

As their investments grew, so did their obsession with the crypto world. They found themselves constantly glued to their screens, anxiously monitoring price movements and devouring news updates in search of the next big opportunity.

But their excitement soon turned to dismay when they fell victim to a cunning crypto scam, losing a staggering 15 lakh rupees in a single ill-fated investment. The rug had been pulled out from. they uncovered a tangled web of deceit and deception that sent shockwaves through the entire industry. Behind the glossy veneer of promise and potential lurked a shadowy underworld of scams and schemes designed to prey upon the unsuspecting and the hopeful.

Their once-solid friendship began to strain under the weight of their shared obsession, as disagreements over investment strategies and risk tolerance drove a wedge between them. Where once they had been united in their pursuit of wealth, now they found themselves at odds, each blaming the other for their mounting losses.

And then, the unthinkable happened. The crypto scam that had once seemed like a distant threat became a harsh reality, as Kiran and Techy watched helplessly as their savings evaporated before their eyes. The devastating blow of financial ruin left them reeling, their dreams shattered and their future uncertain.

As they struggled to come to terms with their losses, Kiran and Techy were forced to confront the toll that their obsession with wealth had taken on their lives. They realized that they had become so fixated on the promise of riches that they had lost sight of what truly mattered: their relationships, their happiness, and their sense of self-worth.

In the aftermath of their ordeal, Kiran and Techy made a conscious decision to reassess their priorities. They vowed to prioritize their personal well-being over their pursuit of wealth, to mend the fractured bonds of friendship that had been strained by their obsession with money, and to find fulfillment in life beyond the relentless pursuit of financial gain.

It was a painful lesson, but one that ultimately led Kiran and Techy to a newfound sense of perspective and purpose. As they slowly began to rebuild their lives, they found solace in the knowledge that true wealth lay not in the pursuit of money, but in the richness of their relationships and the depth of their connections with others.

Their journey took them to the dark corners of the internet, where they encountered ruthless scammers peddling fraudulent meme coins and Web3 gaming platforms promising unimaginable riches with a single click. With each revelation, their determination to expose the truth only grew stronger, fueled by a sense of righteous anger and a desire to protect others from falling victim to the same fate. In the end they filled a complaint against virtual scammers under cybercrime and hopefully doing research for getting thier money back.

CHAPTER 7: SOUMYA'S SETBACK

The Virtual Trap

Soumya Sharma sat at her desk, sipping her morning coffee and scrolling through her emails. Among the usual barrage of promotional offers and work-related messages, one email caught her eye. It was from her bank, or so it seemed.

The subject line read: "Urgent: Verify Your Account Information." Soumya's heart skipped a beat. She clicked on the email, her curiosity piqued by the sense of urgency conveyed in the subject line.

The email appeared to be from her bank, complete with the logo and branding she recognized. It stated that there had been suspicious activity detected on her account and that she needed to verify her information to prevent any unauthorized access.

Without thinking, Soumya clicked on the link provided in the email and was directed to a website that looked exactly like her bank's official website. She entered her login credentials, believing she was taking the necessary steps to protect her account.

Satisfied that she had done her due diligence, Soumya went about her day, unaware of the trap she had just fallen into.

Days passed, and Soumya noticed nothing out of the ordinary until she received a notification from her bank alerting her to unusual activity on her account. Panic set in as she realized that she had been a victim of cyber fraud.

Frantically, Soumya contacted her bank and explained the situation. It was then that she learned the harsh truth - the email she had received was a phishing scam, designed to trick unsuspecting victims into divulging their personal information.

As Soumya delved deeper into the details of the scam, she discovered the various components that made it so convincing and effective.

The Anatomy of a Phishing Scam:

1. The Spoofed Email Address: The email appeared to be from Soumya's bank, complete with the bank's logo and branding. However, upon closer inspection, she realized that the email address was slightly different from the official bank domain.

2. The Sense of Urgency: The subject line of the email conveyed a sense of urgency, urging Soumya to take immediate action to verify her account information. This sense of urgency is a common tactic used by scammers to elicit a quick response from their victims.

3. The Fake Website: The link provided in the email directed Soumya to a website that looked exactly like her bank's official website. However, upon closer

inspection, she noticed subtle differences in the URL and layout of the page.

4. The Request for Personal Information: Once on the fake website, Soumya was prompted to enter her login credentials to verify her account. Unaware that she was being deceived, she willingly entered her information, believing she was taking the necessary steps to protect her account.

5. The Consequences of Falling Victim: It wasn't until Soumya received a notification from her bank alerting her to unusual activity on her account that she realized she had been scammed. By then, it was too late, and the damage had already been done.

As Soumya grappled with the aftermath of the phishing scam, she couldn't help but feel a sense of betrayal and violation. She had trusted the email because it looked so legitimate, only to discover later that it was a fake.

Determined to prevent others from falling victim to similar scams, Soumya decided to share her story and educate others about the dangers of phishing. She reached out to her friends and family, warning them to be vigilant and skeptical of unsolicited emails requesting personal information.

In the end, Soumya emerged from the ordeal wiser and more cautious than before. She had learned the hard way that in the digital age, trust must be earned, and even the most legitimate-looking emails can be deceiving.ultimately she filled a complaint against scam in cyber crime branch.

CHAPTER 8: SHIKSHA-SHADOWS OF DECEPTION

Shiksha, a talented model and aspiring actor, stood on the brink of realizing her dreams in the glitzy world of Bollywood. However, financial constraints threatened to derail her aspirations, particularly when she needed funds for her portfolio shoot.

Despite her efforts, Shiksha's low credit score hindered her ability to secure a loan from traditional sources. Feeling desperate, she turned to online loan apps, hoping for a quick solution to her financial woes.

One such app caught her eye, offering instant approval and disbursal of funds. With optimism and a touch of apprehension, Shiksha applied, consenting to the app's request for access to her phone's sensitive data, including contacts and gallery.

The loan was swiftly granted, and Shiksha breathed a sigh of relief as she embarked on her portfolio shoot. Little did she know, however, that she had unwittingly entered into a web of deceit and manipulation.

As time passed, Shiksha received a shockingly high interest bill from the loan provider. Struggling to make repayments, she found herself harassed by aggressive recovery agents, demanding immediate payment of the mounting debt.

Despite her efforts to negotiate and explain her situation, the agents showed no mercy, resorting to intimidation and threats to coerce her into paying up. Fearing for her safety and reputation, Shiksha felt trapped and helpless, her world crumbling around her.

In her darkest moment, Shiksha contemplated taking drastic action to end her life, but fate intervened in the form of her devoted boyfriend. Sensing her distress, he intervened and prevented her from harming herself, offering unwavering support and love in her time of need.

Together, Shiksha and her boyfriend took a stand against the harassment, filing a complaint and launching an investigation into the online loan scam. With determination and perseverance, they uncovered a sophisticated network of cybercriminals operating from abroad, with links to cross-border.

As they delved deeper into the complex world of cybercrime, Shiksha and her boyfriend gathered evidence and built a case against the scammers. With the help of cybercrime agencies, they worked tirelessly to bring the criminals to justice, ensuring that others would not fall victim to their schemes, she found solace in knowing that she had stood up for herself and fought back against the shadows of deception.

CHAPTER 9: THE BATTLE BEGINS

The Strategy:Uniting Against the Virtual Vipers

In Mumbai, Rajeev sat at his computer, his eyes glued to the screen as he sifted through emails and messages. His heart raced with anticipation as he opened a new message, hoping for a glimmer of hope in his battle against the virtual vipers.

Meanwhile, in Gurgaon, Mohit stared at his phone, his mind swirling with confusion and frustration. He had fallen victim to the cunning schemes of the virtual vipers, losing his hard-earned money in the blink of an eye. But now, as he scrolled through online forums and chat rooms, he felt a flicker of hope ignite within him. Perhaps, he thought, he was not alone in his fight against the cybercriminals.

In city of Joy Kolkata, Riya sat in her office, her fingers flying across the keyboard as she researched the latest developments in cybercrime. As a journalist, she had seen firsthand the devastating impact of online scams and frauds, and she was determined to shine a light on the shadowy world of the virtual vipers.

In Delhi, Ravi paced back and forth in his office, his mind racing with thoughts of revenge and justice. He had dedicated his life to helping others through his

NGO, but now he found himself a victim of the very same criminals he had sworn to fight against. With a steely resolve, he vowed to bring the virtual vipers to justice, no matter the cost.

As the sun set over the city of Bangalore, Jyoti sat alone in her apartment, her eyes brimming with tears as she stared at her bank statement. She had fallen for the promises of easy money and quick riches, only to find herself ensnared in a web of deceit and betrayal. But as she wiped away her tears and opened her laptop, she knew that she was not alone in her struggle.

In the suburbs of Hyderabad, Kiran sat at his kitchen table, his hands trembling with anger as he read through the latest news articles about cybercrime. He had lost everything to the virtual vipers - his savings, his reputation, his sense of security. But now, as he connected with others who had suffered the same fate, he felt a renewed sense of purpose stir within him.

In Chennai, Soumya sat in her bedroom, her heart heavy with regret as she replayed the events of the past few months in her mind. She had fallen for the promises of easy money, only to find herself trapped in a nightmare of debt and despair. But now, as she reached out to others who had been through similar experiences, she felt a glimmer of hope begin to bloom within her.

And finally, in Mumbai, Shiksha sat at her desk, her eyes filled with determination as she stared at her computer screen. She had been through hell and back, but now she was ready to take a stand against the virtual vipers and reclaim her life once and for all.

As the night stretched on, the eight strangers from across India connected online, their voices mingling in a chorus of determination and resolve. They shared their stories, their fears, their hopes, and their dreams, united in their fight against the virtual vipers.

With each passing moment, their bond grew stronger, as they exchanged information, shared resources, and offered support to one another. They knew that they faced an uphill battle against powerful and cunning adversaries, but they also knew that together, they were unstoppable.

Weeks turned into months, and the group worked tirelessly to gather evidence, track down leads, and expose the virtual vipers for the criminals they truly were. They combed through mountains of data, piecing together the intricate web of deception that had ensnared them all.

As they delved deeper into the world of cybercrime, they encountered countless obstacles and challenges along the way. They faced off against ruthless adversaries, dodged traps and pitfalls, and risked everything to uncover the truth.

But with each setback came a renewed sense of determination, as they refused to be deterred by the forces arrayed against them. They knew that they were fighting for more than just themselves - they were fighting for justice, for truth, and for the countless others who had fallen victim to the virtual vipers' schemes.

And then, one fateful day, their perseverance paid off. They uncovered a crucial piece of evidence that connected the virtual vipers to a sophisticated network of cybercriminals operating from abroad. With the evidence in hand, they reached out to cybercrime experts and law enforcement agencies, presenting their findings and demanding action against the perpetrators.

The authorities, impressed by the group's diligence and dedication, launched a full-scale investigation into the cybercrime syndicate, mobilizing resources to dismantle their operations and apprehend those responsible. With each passing day, the net drew tighter around the virtual vipers, until finally, they were brought to justice , a wave of relief washed over the group, as they realized that they had finally won their battle against the virtual vipers. Though their journey had been long and arduous, they emerged victorious, their spirits unbroken and their resolve unwavering in the face of adversity.

And as they reflected on their journey, Rajeev, Mohit, Riya, Ravi, Jyoti, Kiran, Soumya, and Shiksha knew that they had made a difference. Their courage and determination had not only saved themselves from further harm but had also exposed the dark underbelly of cybercrime and paved the way for a safer digital world.

Together, they had turned the tables on the virtual vipers, proving that when ordinary people come together for a common cause, they can achieve the extraordinary. And though their journey had been fraught with danger and uncertainty, they emerged stronger, wiser, and more united than ever before.

CHAPTER 10: THE ROAD TO JUSTICE

The Investigation

The victims, united by a sense of betrayal and loss, turned to retired banking security official Vikram and cybercrime expert Neha Sharma and her team for help. Together, they embarked on a mission to solve the mystery and bring the virtual vipers to justice. The Investigation Begins:

Vikram and Neha wasted no time in assembling a team of experts to aid in the investigation. They gathered the victims - Rajeev, Mohit, Riya, Ravi, Soumya, Jyoti, Shiksha , Kiran and many others victims - to share their experiences and piece together the puzzle.

Each victim recounted their harrowing ordeal, detailing how they had fallen prey to the cunning tactics of the cybercriminals. From phishing emails to fraudulent investment schemes, the perpetrators had inflicted left a trail of devastation in their wake. Vikram and Neha listened intently, taking note of commonalities and patterns in the scams.

They identified key components of the operation, including spoofed email addresses which were as original as the genuine email, fake websites exactly same as original and the relentless requests for personal information, cloning ATM cards, credit cards, UPI transfer.

With the code name "Virtual Vipers" assigned to the operation, Vikram and Neha began their pior investigation. They analyzed digital footprints of each communication traced each email,all voice call, exploring chats everything available, traced IP addresses, and combed through financial records in search of clues,these traces drawn them to some IP address and they tried to locate its geographical location and arranged an unofficial reki of that in search of more clues.

Identifying the Money Trail

Neha Sharma and her team gathered financial records from the victims, tracing back the transactions associated with the scams. They scrutinized the account where amount was deposit search bank statements, credit card bills, and transaction histories to identify all suspicious or unauthorized payments related to those unidentified account and traced there location, Vikram the internet banking security experts used all his experience and knowledge trying to link the money trail forward a draws various clues and identify the real operator of the suspicious account.

Using advanced data analysis techniques, the team examined transaction patterns to discern any anomalies or irregularities. They looked for unusual patterns such as large, unexplained transfers or frequent transactions to unfamiliar accounts. Neha and her team followed the money trail forward, starting from the victims' accounts and tracing the flow of funds through various channels. They tracked the movement of money across different accounts and financial institutions, piecing together the route taken by the cybercriminals.

Through their analysis, the team identified common destinations where the funds were ultimately transferred. These footprints include offshore accounts, cryptocurrency exchanges, or other digital payment platforms often favored by cybercriminals for their anonymity and ease of use. These dark web transactions are easy to hide and hard to trace but still following the route in dark web called silk route and dark rooms account tracking footprints on general website links was present.

To corroborate their findings, Neha cross-referenced the financial data with other sources of information, such as IP addresses, email communications,dark web authority and website activity. This helped to establish connections between the financial transactions and the broader cybercriminal network.

Recognizing Digital Footprints

Neha Sharma's team collected digital evidence from various sources, including email servers, web servers, and internet service providers. They retrieved logs, metadata, and other digital artifacts that could provide insights into the activities of the cybercriminals. Using specialized forensic tools and techniques, the team analyzed the collected data to identify digital footprints left behind by the cybercriminals. This involved examining email headers, server logs, and network traffic to trace the origin and movement of digital communications. Neha's team traced IP addresses associated with suspicious activities, such as phishing emails or fraudulent website visits. They used geolocation data to map out the physical locations linked to these IP addresses, providing valuable clues about the whereabouts of the cybercriminals. They traced mobile records and find the adhar address mentioned to the allotted numbers. The team conducted in-depth analysis of the fake websites used by the cybercriminals, looking for telltale signs of manipulation or deception. This included examining HTML code, server configurations, and domain registration information to uncover the identities of the website operators.

By comparing digital footprints across different scams and incidents, Neha's team identified common patterns and techniques used by the cybercriminals. This allowed them to build a comprehensive profile of the perpetrators and their modus operandi.Small raids conducted on fake call centre and interrogation with fake employees give them valuable insights about actuall size of crime. Neha Sharma and her team employed a combination of forensic analysis, data mining, and investigative techniques to identify the money trail and recognize digital footprints left by the cybercriminals

The Breakthrough

Through collaborative efforts with international law enforcement agencies—IB, FBI, Scotland Yard, Chinese police, and CIA—a global network emerged to combat the Virtual Vipers. Cooperation across borders was essential as they pieced together the puzzle, pooling expertise to disrupt the syndicate.Months of dogged determination culminated in a series of coordinated takedowns. Across continents, simultaneous operations unfolded as authorities moved to apprehend those responsible. The web of deceit began to unravel, exposing the individuals and entities behind the fraudulent schemes.For the victims, justice was long overdue.

Retired banking security official Vikram and cybercrime expert Neha Sharma wasted no time assembling a team of experts from various fields including cybersecurity, financial analysis, and law enforcement of different countries and lead a international collaboration they raid across border simultaneously and arrested many scammers and then a series of interrogation peeled each layer of crime just like a twisted tale came to end.

Apprehending the cybercriminals and dismantling their operation. As news of the takedown spread, the victims found solace in knowing that justice had been served. Though the scars of their ordeal would linger, they knew their voices had been heard, and their perpetrators held accountable.

The cybercriminals utilized spoofed email addresses to deceive victims into providing sensitive information or clicking on malicious links. They created fake websites mimicking legitimate institutions to lure victims into fraudulent schemes, such as investment scams or phishing schemes. The scammers employed social engineering tactics to trick victims into divulging personal information, which they then used for identity theft or further fraudulent activities.

The investigation uncovered the various channels used by the cybercriminals to transfer money, including cryptocurrency exchanges and offshore accounts, complicating the tracing process. Vikram, Neha, and their team adopted a collaborative approach, leveraging expertise from multiple domains to piece together the puzzle.

Through digital forensics, they traced the digital footprints and they identified the individuals and entities involved in the fraudulent schemes, unraveling the conspiracy,that displaced many lifes,hard rock for economy of country, traumatized individuals and looting there hard earn money,these vipers spited thier venom on lifes of everyone who is surfing internet. The dark web connection of vipers is a safe wall to hide , but Neha approach and dedication has busted these racket of vipers. Collaboration with law enforcement agencies and cybercrime units was crucial in gathering evidence and executing the takedown operation, ensuring the perpetrators faced justice.

The Takedown: After months of relentless pursuit, Vikram and Neha finally had enough evidence to take down the virtual vipers once and for all. With the support of law enforcement, they executed a series of coordinated raids, apprehending the cybercriminals and dismantling their operation. As news of the takedown spread, the victims breathed a sigh of relief. Though the scars of their ordeal would linger, they found solace in knowing that their voices had been heard and their perpetrators had been held accountable.Those who had bravely filed complaints against cybercrime saw their efforts vindicated as funds were recovered and restitution began. Relief washed over them, their hard-earned money and peace of mind restored.Neha Sharma stood at the forefront, a beacon of resilience against the darkness of cybercrime. Her dedication and unwavering resolve had shattered the illusion of invincibility cultivated by the Virtual Vipers. With each arrest, each piece of evidence unearthed, she drew closer to dismantling the syndicate entirely.The epilogue of this saga was not just about the apprehension of criminals—it was a testament to the resilience of humanity against digital predators. The collaboration between Vikram, Neha, and their global allies underscored the power of unity in combating transnational crime.

CHAPTER 11: THE FIGHT AGAINST CYBERCRIME

The Awareness Campaign

Introduction to all types of scams

Sure, let's break down each mentioned scam, simplify its identification, provide remedies, and list relevant helplines in the context of India:

1.Ponzi Schemes:

- Identification: Ponzi schemes promise high returns with little or no risk, relying on funds from new investors to pay returns to earlier investors.

- Remedies: Report the scheme to the Securities and Exchange Board of India (SEBI) or the Economic Offences Wing (EOW) of the police.

- Helpline:SEBI Investor Helpline: 1800-266-7575

2. Pyramid Schemes:

- Identification: Pyramid schemes recruit members to buy into a program, with promises of payments for recruiting others into the scheme rather than selling actual products or services.

- Remedies: File a complaint with the Ministry of Corporate Affairs or the Competition Commission of India (CCI).

- Helpline: CCI Helpline: 1800-112-100

3. Investment Fraud:

- Identification: Investment fraud involves false promises of high returns with low risk, often through fake investment opportunities or unregistered schemes.

-Remedies: Report the fraud to SEBI, EOW, or the Reserve Bank of India (RBI).

- Helpline: RBI Complaints: 1800-266-3370

4. Stock Market Manipulation:

- Identification: Stock market manipulation involves artificially inflating or deflating stock prices through false information, rumors, or illegal trading practices.

- Remedies:Report the manipulation to SEBI or the Securities Fraud Investigation Office (SFIO).

- Helpline: SFIO Helpline: 1800-111-364

5.High-Yield Investment Programs (HYIPs):

-Identification: HYIPs promise unrealistically high returns on investments, often using funds from new investors to pay returns to earlier investors.

- Remedies: File a complaint with SEBI or EOW.

-Helpline: EOW Helpline: Contact your local police station.

6. Binary Options Scams:

- Identification: Binary options scams promise high returns on investments by predicting the price movement of assets, but often result in losses due to rigged platforms or false advertising.

- Remedies: Report the scam to SEBI or EOW.

- Helpline: SEBI Complaints: 1800-266-7575

7. Forex Trading Scams:

- Identification: Forex trading scams involve fraudulent brokers or platforms that manipulate trades, misappropriate funds, or engage in deceptive practices.

- Remedies: File a complaint with SEBI or the National Consumer Helpline.

- Helpline: National Consumer Helpline: 1800-11-4000

8. Cryptocurrency Scams:

-Identification: Cryptocurrency scams include fake ICOs, Ponzi schemes, fake wallets, and phishing scams targeting cryptocurrency investors.

-Remedies: Report the scam to SEBI or the Cyber Crime Cell of the police.

- Helpline: Cyber Crime Cell Helpline: Contact your local police station.

9.Advance Fee Fraud:

- Identification: Advance fee fraud involves requesting upfront payments or fees in exchange for promised rewards, such as lottery winnings, loans, or job offers.

- Remedies: File a complaint with the Cyber Crime Cell of the police or the Consumer Helpline.

- Helpline: Consumer Helpline: 1800-11-4000

10.Phishing Scams

- Identification: Phishing scams use deceptive emails, websites, or messages to trick individuals into revealing personal information or financial details.

- Remedies: Report the phishing attempt to the Cyber Crime Cell or the Anti-Phishing Working Group (APWG).

- Helpline: Cyber Crime Cell Helpline: Contact your local police station.

CHAPTER 12
THE PRECAUTIONS

Protect Your Card Information:

- Guard Your Card: Keep your credit card physically secure and never share your card details, such as the card number, expiration date, or CVV code, with anyone you don't trust.

- Secure Transactions: Only use your credit card on secure websites with HTTPS encryption and avoid providing card information over unsecured or unfamiliar channels.

Enable Fraud Alerts:

- Activate Alerts: Set up fraud alerts or notifications with your credit card issuer to receive alerts for suspicious activity, such as large transactions or transactions in unusual locations.

-Immediate Action:If you receive a fraud alert, contact your credit card issuer immediately to confirm the legitimacy of the transaction and take appropriate action if it's fraudulent.

Use Strong Passwords and Authentication:

-Secure Account Access: Use strong, unique passwords at least 16bit for your online accounts and enable two-factor authentication (2FA) to add an extra layer of security to your credit card accounts.

-Prevent Unauthorized Access: By securing your account credentials, you can reduce the risk of unauthorized access to your credit card information.

Regularly Check Credit Reports:

- Review Credit Reports: Monitor your credit report regularly to check for any suspicious activity or unauthorized accounts that could indicate identity theft or credit card fraud.

- Dispute Errors: If you spot any inaccuracies or fraudulent accounts on your credit report, dispute them with the credit bureau and take steps to protect your credit.

Report Lost or Stolen Cards Immediately:

- Prompt Action: If your credit card is lost or stolen, report it to your credit card issuer immediately to have the card canceled and request a replacement.

- Monitor for Fraudulent Activity:Keep an eye on your account for any unauthorized charges that may occur as a result of the lost or stolen card.

By following these proactive measures and staying vigilant, you can reduce the risk of falling victim to credit card scams and take swift action to resolve any fraudulent activity if it occurs.

CHAPTER 13
IDENTIFYING RED FLAGS

In the digital age, scams abound, lurking behind the guise of legitimacy. Whether you're browsing the web, checking your email, or using social media, it's crucial to be vigilant. Here are ten red flags to help you identify a scammer online:

Too Good to Be True Offers: If an offer seems too good to be true, it probably is. Scammers often entice victims with unrealistic promises of quick money, luxurious prizes, or unbelievable discounts.

Unsolicited Communication: Be wary of unsolicited emails, messages, or phone calls, especially if they pressure you to act urgently or disclose personal information.

Poor Grammar and Spelling: Many scams originate from non-native English speakers or hastily put-together operations, leading to noticeable errors in grammar and spelling.

Requests for Personal Information: Legitimate organizations rarely request sensitive information like passwords, Social Security numbers, or bank details via email or message. Treat any such requests with suspicion.

Phishing Links: Beware of links in emails or messages that direct you to unfamiliar websites asking for login credentials or financial details. Always verify the legitimacy of the website before entering any information.

Pressure Tactics: Scammers often use pressure tactics to rush victims into making impulsive decisions. Be cautious of anyone who insists on immediate action or threatens negative consequences for hesitating.

Untraceable Payment Methods: Scammers prefer untraceable payment methods like wire transfers, cryptocurrency, or gift cards. Avoid transactions that lack accountability or recourse.

Inconsistencies in Branding: Check for inconsistencies in logos, branding, or domain names. Scammers may mimic reputable brands with slight alterations to deceive unsuspecting victims.

Lack of Transparency: Legitimate businesses provide clear information about their products, services, and contact details. If you encounter evasiveness or vague responses, proceed with caution.

Trust Your Instincts: Ultimately, trust your instincts. If something feels off or too good to be true, take a step back and conduct further research before proceeding.

"Signs That Someone May Be Trying to Scam You in Person"

While online scams grab headlines, scammers also operate in the physical world, preying on unsuspecting individuals through various schemes. Here are some signs to watch for to identify potential scams in person:

High-Pressure Sales Tactics: Beware of salespeople who use high-pressure tactics to coerce you into making a purchase or signing a contract on the spot. Legitimate businesses respect your decision-making process and allow time for consideration

Fake Charities: Scammers may pose as representatives of charitable organizations, soliciting donations for fake causes. Research charities independently and donate directly to reputable organizations to avoid falling victim to fraudulent schemes.

False Emergency Scenarios: Be skeptical of strangers claiming to be in distress or experiencing emergencies, especially if they request immediate financial assistance. Verify the situation independently before offering any aid.

Impersonation of Authority Figures: Scammers may impersonate authority figures such as law enforcement officers, government officials, or utility workers to gain your trust. Always ask for identification and verify their credentials before complying with any requests.

Overpayment Scams: Exercise caution when dealing with transactions involving overpayment, especially if the buyer insists on reimbursing you with a larger sum and requesting a refund for the difference. This tactic often involves counterfeit checks or stolen credit cards.

Unsolicited Home Repairs: Be wary of individuals offering unsolicited home repair services, especially if they claim to have noticed issues that require immediate attention. Always research contractors and obtain multiple quotes before agreeing to any repairs.

Prize or Lottery Scams: If you receive notifications claiming you've won a prize or lottery you never entered, proceed with skepticism. Legitimate contests do not require upfront fees or personal information to claim winnings.

Unsolicited Investment Opportunities: Exercise caution when approached with unsolicited investment opportunities promising high returns with little to no risk.Always conduct thorough research and seek advice from trusted financial professionals before investing your money.

"Recognizing Common Signs of Phone Scams and How to Respond"

Phone scams remain a persistent threat in today's interconnected world, with scammers employing various tactics to deceive unsuspecting individuals. Recognizing the signs of phone scams is essential for safeguarding yourself against potential financial loss or identity theft. Here are common signs of phone scams and how to respond

Call Forwarding this is also a crucial thing to be aware of always check by dialling*#62# that no call forwarding is active in your handset and to stop call forwarding at once dial##002# this will reset your device call setting.

Always remember be aware and remain vigilant.

Caller ID Spoofing: Scammers often manipulate caller ID information to make it appear as though they're calling from a legitimate organization or government agency. If you receive a call from an unfamiliar number, exercise caution, and verify the caller's identity before divulging any personal information.

Threats and Intimidation: Scammers may use intimidation tactics, such as threatening legal action, arrest, or the suspension of services, to coerce victims into complying with their demands. Remember that legitimate entities do not resort to intimidation over the phone, and never provide sensitive information to unsolicited callers.

Requests for Personal Information: Be wary of callers who request personal information such as Social Security numbers, bank account details, or passwords over the phone. Legitimate organizations typically do not ask for sensitive information during unsolicited calls.

Unsolicited Tech Support Calls: Beware of unsolicited calls from individuals claiming to be tech support representatives. These scammers may attempt to gain remote access to your computer or trick you into installing malicious software.

Robocalls and Automated Messages: Robocalls deliver pre-recorded messages designed to elicit a response from recipients. Hang up immediately if you receive a robocall, as legitimate businesses typically do not rely on automated messages for customer communication.

Unsolicited Investment Opportunities: Exercise caution if you receive unsolicited calls promoting investment opportunities with guaranteed returns or low-risk propositions.

Trust Your Instincts: If something feels off or too good to be true, trust your instincts. Do not hesitate to end the call and report suspicious activity to the appropriate authorities.

Ministry of Home Affairs

Cases of Cyber Frauds

Posted On: 06 FEB 2024 5:45PM by PIB Delhi

The National Crime Records Bureau (NCRB) compiles and publishes the statistical data on crimes in its publication "Crime in India". The latest published report is for the year 2022.

'Police' and 'Public Order' are State subjects as per the Seventh Schedule of the Constitution of India. States/UTs are primarily responsible for the prevention, detection, investigation and prosecution of cyber crimes through their Law Enforcement Agencies. The Central Government supplements the initiatives of the State Governments through advisories and schemes for the capacity building of their Law Enforcement Agencies. To strengthen the mechanism to deal with cyber crimes in a comprehensive and coordinated manner, the Central Government, through Ministry of Home Affairs has set up the 'Indian Cyber Crime Coordination Centre' (I4C) to deal with all types of cyber crime in the country.

The 'National Cyber Crime Reporting Portal' (https://cybercrime.gov.in) has been launched, as a part of the I4C, to enable public to report incidents pertaining to all types of cyber crimes, with special focus on cyber crimes against women and children. Cyber crime incidents reported on this portal, their conversion into FIRs and subsequent action thereon are handled by the State/UT Law Enforcement Agencies concerned as per the provisions of the law. The 'Citizen Financial Cyber Fraud Reporting and Management System', under I4C, has been launched for immediate reporting of financial frauds and to stop siphoning off funds by the fraudsters. Since inception of Citizen Financial Cyber Fraud Reporting and Management System, more than Rs. 1200 Crore have been saved in more than 4.7 lakh complaints. A toll-free Helpline number '1930' has been operationalized to get assistance in lodging online cyber complaints. The State/UT wise details of Citizen Financial Cyber Fraud Reporting Management System during the period 1.1.2023 to 31.12.2023 are at the Annexure. Till date more than 3.2 lakhs SIM cards and 49,000 IMEIs as reported by Police authorities have been blocked by Government of India.

CERT-In issues alerts and advisories regarding latest cyber threats/vulnerabilities and countermeasures to protect computers, mobile phones, networks and data on an ongoing basis. CERT-In, through RBI, has advised all authorised entities and banks issuing pre-paid payment instruments (wallets) in the country to carry out special audit by CERT-In-empanelled auditors, close the non-compliances identified in the audit report and ensure implementation of security best practices. CERT-In and the Reserve Bank of India (RBI) jointly carry out a cyber security awareness campaign on 'beware and be aware of financial frauds' through the Digital India Platform.

To spread awareness on cyber crime, the Central Government has taken steps which, inter-alia, include; dissemination of messages through SMS, I4C social media account i.e. X (formerly Twitter) (@Cyberdost), Facebook(CyberDostI4C), Instagram (cyberdostI4C), Telegram (cyberdosti4c), Radio campaign, engaged MyGov for publicity in multiple mediums, organizing Cyber Safety and Security Awareness weeks in association with States/UTs, publishing of Handbook for Adolescents/Students, etc. The States/UTs have also been requested to carry out publicity to create mass awareness.

State/UT wise details of Citizen Financial Cyber Fraud Reporting Management System during the period 1.1.2023 to 31.12.2023

ANNEXURE

Sl. No.	State	No of Complaint Reported	Amount Reported (Rs in Lacs)	No of Complaints (Put on Hold)	Lien Amount (Rs in Lacs)
1	Andaman & Nicobar	526	311.97	161	26.46
2	Andhra Pradesh	33507	37419.77	9580	4664.14
3	Arunachal Pradesh	470	765.79	127	34.39
4	Assam	7621	3441.8	2163	451.61
5	Bihar	42029	24327.79	11533	2779.41
6	Chandigarh	3601	2258.61	1058	296.67
7	Chhattisgarh	18147	8777.15	5056	898.41
8	Dadra & Nagar Haveli and Daman & Diu	412	326.21	105	40.88
9	Delhi	58748	39157.86	13674	3425.03
10	Goa	1788	2318.25	450	153.22
11	Gujarat	121701	65053.35	49220	15690.9
12	Haryana	76736	41924.75	21178	4653.4
13	Himachal Pradesh	5268	4115.25	1502	370.78
14	Jammu & Kashmir	1046	786.56	253	62.55
15	Jharkhand	10040	6788.98	2822	556.38
16	Karnataka	64301	66210.02	18989	7315.52
17	Kerala	23757	20179.86	8559	3647.83

18	Ladakh	162	190.29	41	10.03
19	Lakshadweep	29	19.58	6	0.51
20	Madhya Pradesh	37435	19625.03	9336	1462.33
21	Maharashtra	125153	99069.22	32050	10308.47
22	Manipur	339	333.03	108	66.94
23	Meghalaya	654	424.2	252	46.71
24	Mizoram	239	484.12	75	35.44
25	Nagaland	224	148.94	73	18.09
26	Odisha	16869	7967.11	5187	1049.34
27	Puducherry	1953	2020.34	568	143.38
28	Punjab	19252	12178.42	4923	1332.66
29	Rajasthan	77769	35392.09	20899	3934.82
30	Sikkim	292	197.92	65	18.01
31	Tamil Nadu	59549	66123.21	17941	6980.72
32	Telangana	71426	75905.62	26148	13137.94
33	Tripura	1913	900.35	488	84.82
34	Uttarakhand	17958	6879.67	4813	708.94
35	Uttar Pradesh	197547	72107.46	44089	5906.86
36	West Bengal	29804	24733.33	6307	1845.97
	Total	**1128265**	**748863.9**	**319799**	**92159.56**

This was stated by the Minister of State for Home Affairs, Shri Ajay Kumar Mishra in a written reply to a question in the Lok Sabha.

As reported by pib.gov.in on 06-02-2024 NEW DELHI

CHAPTER 14
THE INFINITY IN CYBERCRIME

1. Hacking

-**Description**: Unauthorized access to computer systems or networks.

Example: An individual gaining access to a company's confidential database to steal sensitive information such as customer data or proprietary business plans.

Punishment (India) Under Section 66 of the IT Act, 2000, this crime can result in imprisonment for up to three years and/or a fine up to Rs. 5 lakh.

2. Cyberbullying

Description: Using digital platforms to harass, threaten, or intimidate individuals.

Example: Sending threatening messages or spreading rumors about someone on social media to cause emotional distress.

Punishment (India): Under Section 67 of the IT Act, 2000, cyberbullying can lead to imprisonment for up to three years and a fine up to Rs. 5 lakh.

3. Spamming

Description: Sending unsolicited bulk messages for advertising purposes.

Example: Receiving numerous unsolicited emails promoting a product or service, often from unknown sources.

Punishment (India): Penalties under various sections of the IT Act, generally imprisonment up to three years and fines.

4. Phishing

Description: Fraudulent attempts to obtain sensitive information by disguising as a trustworthy entity.

Example: Fake emails pretending to be from a bank asking for login credentials or credit card information.

Punishment (India): Under Section 66C of the IT Act, 2000, this crime can result in imprisonment for up to three years and a fine up to Rs. 1 lakh.

5. Virus Attack

Description: Malicious software designed to damage or disrupt computer systems.

Example: A computer virus that deletes files or encrypts data, rendering the system inoperable until a ransom is paid.

Punishment (India): Under Section 66 of the IT Act, 2000, this offense can lead to imprisonment for up to three years and/or a fine up to Rs. 5 lakh.

6. Vulgar Content

Description: Distributing or publishing obscene or offensive content digitally.

Example: Sharing explicit images or videos without the consent of the individuals involved.

Punishment (India): Under Section 67 of the IT Act, 2000, first-time offenders can face imprisonment for up to three years and a fine up to Rs. 5 lakh.

7. Child Pornography

Description: Creating, distributing, or possessing sexually explicit material involving minors.

Example: Downloading or sharing images or videos of child exploitation.

Punishment (India): Under the POCSO Act, this crime can result in imprisonment ranging from five years to life, with fines.

8.Hate Speech

Description: Using digital platforms to incite violence or hatred against individuals or groups based on race, religion, ethnicity, etc.

Example: Posting messages that promote violence against a particular community on social media.

Punishment (India): Under Section 153A of IPC, this crime can lead to imprisonment for up to three years and/or a fine.

9.Blackmailing

Description: Threatening to release sensitive or embarrassing information unless a demand is met.

Example: Threatening to release private photos or information unless a ransom is paid.

Punishment (India): Under Section 66E of the IT Act, 2000, this offense can result in imprisonment for up to three years or a fine up to Rs. 2 lakh.

10. Identity Theft

Description: Unauthorized use of someone's personal information to commit fraud or other crimes.

Example: Using stolen personal details to open credit card accounts or apply for loans in someone else's name.

Punishment (India): Under Section 66C of the IT Act, 2000, this crime can lead to imprisonment for up to three years and a fine up to Rs. 1 lakh.

11. Ransomware Attacks

Description: Malicious software that encrypts data and demands payment for the decryption key.

Example: A ransomware attack encrypting a hospital's patient records and demanding a ransom to restore access.

Punishment (India): Covered under Section 66 of the IT Act, 2000, similar to hacking offenses.

12.Denial of Service (DoS) and Distributed Denial of Service (DDoS) Attacks

Description: Overwhelming a website or service with traffic, rendering it unavailable.

Example: Crashing an online retailer's website by flooding it with traffic during a major sale.

Punishment (India): Addressed under various sections of the IT Act.

13. Spyware and Keyloggers

Description: Malicious software that monitors user activity and captures keystrokes to steal sensitive information.

Example: A keylogger installed on a computer captures login credentials for online banking sites.

Punishment (India): Under Section 66 of the IT Act, 2000, this can result in imprisonment and fines.

14.Eavesdropping and Man-in-the-Middle (MitM) Attacks

Description: Intercepting and manipulating communication between two parties without their knowledge.

Example: Intercepting communications between a user and their bank, altering transactions to divert funds.

Punishment (India): Addressed under various sections of the IT Act.

15. Cryptojacking

Description: Unauthorized use of someone's computer to mine cryptocurrency.

Example: A malicious script injected into a website using visitors' CPUs to mine cryptocurrency without their consent.

Punishment (India): Covered under Section 66 of the IT Act, 2000, similar to other hacking offenses.

16.Financial Fraud

Description: Conducting fraudulent activities to steal money or financial information.

Example: Creating fake online stores to capture credit card information from unsuspecting buyers.

Punishment (India): Under Sections 420 and 468 of IPC, this crime can lead to imprisonment and fines.

17. Online Scams and Fraud

Description: Deceiving individuals through fraudulent schemes over the internet.

Example: Promising high returns on investments in non-existent cryptocurrencies.

Punishment (India): Addressed under various sections of IPC.

18. Software Piracy

Description: Unauthorized copying, distribution, or use of software.

Example: Downloading and using pirated versions of commercial software.

Punishment (India): Covered under copyright laws and the IT Act.

19. Online Stalking and Harassment

Description: Persistent and unwanted attention or monitoring of individuals online.

Example: Sending repeated threatening messages to someone through social media platforms.

Punishment (India): Addressed under Sections 354D and 509 of IPC.

20. Credit Card Fraud

Description: Unauthorized use of credit card information to make purchases or withdraw money.

Example: Stealing credit card details via a data breach and using them for online shopping.

Punishment (India): Under Section 420 of IPC, this crime can lead to imprisonment and fines.

21. Pharming

Description: Redirecting a website's traffic to a fraudulent site to steal information.

Example: Users attempting to visit their bank's website are redirected to a fake site that looks identical to the real one.

Punishment (India): Addressed under Section 66D of the IT Act, 2000.

22. Cyber Espionage

Description : Unauthorized spying to gain information, often related to government or corporate secrets.

Example: Hacking into a government database to obtain classified information.

Punishment (India): Covered under Section 66F of the IT Act, 2000, with life imprisonment for cyber terrorism.

23. Online Marketplaces for Illegal Goods

Description: Websites or platforms facilitating the sale of illegal goods and services.

Example: Dark web marketplaces where users can buy drugs, weapons, or stolen data.

Punishment (India): Addressed under various sections of the IT Act and IPC.

24. Swatting

Description: Falsely reporting a serious incident to emergency services, causing them to respond with significant force.

Example: Calling the police to falsely report a hostage situation at someone's home, leading to a SWAT team intervention.

-

CHAPTER 15
PUNISHMENT (INDIA): ADDRESSED UNDER VARIOUS SECTIONS OF IPC FOR FALSE REPORTING.

Legal Provisions and Punishments

Information Technology Act, 2000 (IT Act)

Section 43: Penalty up to Rs. 1 crore.

Section 66: Imprisonment up to three years and/or fine up to Rs. 5 lakh.

Section 66A: Struck down but similar penalties under other sections.

Section 66B: Imprisonment up to three years and/or fine up to Rs. 1 lakh.

Section 66C: Imprisonment up to three years and fine up to Rs. 1 lakh for identity theft.

Section 66D: Imprisonment up to three years and/or fine up to Rs. 1 lakh for cheating by personation using computer resources.

Section 66E: Imprisonment up to three years and/or fine up to Rs. 2 lakh for violating privacy.

Section 66F: Life imprisonment for cyber terrorism.

Section 67: Imprisonment up to five years and fine up to Rs. 10 lakh for publishing or transmitting obscene material in electronic form.

Section 67A: Imprisonment up to seven years and fine up to Rs. 10 lakh for publishing or transmitting sexually explicit material.

Section 67B: Imprisonment up to five years and fine up to Rs. 10 lakh for child pornography.

Section 67C: Imprisonment up to three years and fine for failure to preserve records.

Indian Penal Code (IPC)

Section 153A: Imprisonment up to three years and/or fine for promoting enmity between different groups on grounds of religion, race, place of birth, residence, language, etc.

Section 354D: Imprisonment up to three years for stalking.

Section 419: Imprisonment up to three years and/or fine for cheating by personation.

Section 420: Imprisonment up to seven years and fine for cheating and dishonestly inducing delivery of property.

Section 468: Imprisonment up to seven years and fine for forgery for the purpose of cheating.

National Cyber Crime Reporting Portal

Website:cybercrime.gov.in (https://cybercrime.gov.in)

How to File a Complaint

1. Visit the Portal or call at 1930

- Go to [cybercrime.gov.in] (https: / / cybercrime.gov.in).

2. Register/Login:

- Register if you are a new user by providing your details.

- Log in if you are an existing user.

3. Select the Type of Crime:

- Choose the type of cybercrime you want to report, such as cyberbullying, hacking, financial fraud, etc.

4. Fill in the Details:

- Provide necessary details in the complaint form, including personal information, details of the incident, and any evidence like screenshots or messages.

5. Submit the Complaint:

- Submit your complaint after ensuring all required information is filled in.

6. Follow-Up:

- Receive an acknowledgment with a complaint reference number.

- Use this reference number to track the status of your complaint on the portal.

Key Features of the Portal

24/7 Availability: The portal is available online 24/7 for filing complaints.

Anonymous Reporting: Allows for anonymous reporting of child pornography and sexually explicit content.

Grievance Redressal: Provides a mechanism for grievance redressal and updates on the status of the complaint.

Resource Center: Offers resources and information on various types of cybercrimes and how to protect oneself from them.

Additional Assistance

Cyber Crime Cell: Contact your local cyber crime cell for assistance. Each state and major city in India has a dedicated cyber crime cell.

Police Station: Cybercrime complaints can also be filed at the nearest police station. They are obligated to assist in registering your complaint and directing it to the appropriate cybercrime unit.

Steps to Stay Safe Online

1.Use Strong, Unique Passwords:

Description: Create passwords with a mix of upper and lower case letters, numbers, and special characters.

Avoid using easily guessable passwords like "password" or "123456".

Example: Instead of using "john123", use "J0hn!23$!".

Tip: Use a password manager to generate and store unique passwords for each account.

2. Enable Two-Factor Authentication (2FA)

Description: Adds an extra layer of security by requiring a second form of identification beyond just the password.

Example: When logging into your email, after entering your password, you are required to enter a code sent to your mobile phone.

Tip: Enable 2FA on all accounts that offer it, such as email, social media, and banking apps.

3. Keep Software Updated:

Description: Regularly update your operating system, browser, and software to patch vulnerabilities.

Example: Installing the latest updates for your computer's operating system and antivirus software.

Tip: Enable automatic updates to ensure your software is always up-to-date.

4.Be Wary of Phishing Attempts:

Description: Phishing is a fraudulent attempt to obtain sensitive information by disguising as a trustworthy entity.

Example: Receiving an email that looks like it's from your bank asking you to click a link and enter your login details.

Tip: Always verify the sender's email address and avoid clicking on links or downloading attachments from unknown sources.

5. Use Antivirus and Anti-Malware Software:

Description: Install reputable antivirus and anti-malware software to protect your computer from malicious attacks.

Example: Using software like Norton, McAfee, or Kaspersky to scan and protect your system.

Tip: Keep your antivirus software updated and run regular scans.

6. Secure Your Network:

Description: Use a strong password for your Wi-Fi network and change the default settings on your router.

Example: Changing the default Wi-Fi password from "admin" to a more complex password.

Tip: Use WPA3 encryption if available and regularly change your Wi-Fi password.

7. Backup Your Data Regularly:

Description: Regularly back up important data to an external hard drive or cloud storage to prevent data loss.

Example: Saving copies of important documents, photos, and videos to an external hard drive or a cloud service like Google Drive or Dropbox.

Tip: Automate backups to ensure they are done regularly without manual intervention.

8. Limit Personal Information Shared Online:

Description: Be mindful of the personal information you share on social media and other online platforms.

Example: Avoid posting your home address, phone number, or financial information publicly.

Tip: Adjust privacy settings on social media to control who can see your information.

9.Use Secure Connections:

- **Description**: Avoid using public Wi-Fi for sensitive transactions and use a VPN to encrypt your internet connection.

- **Example**: Avoid online banking or shopping over unsecured public Wi-Fi networks.

- **Tip**: Use a reputable VPN service to secure your internet connection, especially when using public Wi-Fi.

10. Monitor Your Accounts:

Description: Regularly review bank and credit card statements for unauthorized transactions.

Example: Checking your bank statements monthly to ensure all transactions are legitimate.

Tip: Set up alerts for unusual activity on your bank accounts and credit cards.

11. Educate Yourself and Others:

Description: Stay informed about the latest cyber threats and educate family members, especially children, about safe online practices.

Example: Teaching children not to share personal information online or click on unknown links.

Tip: Follow trusted sources for cybersecurity news and updates.

12.Enable Firewall:

Description: Ensure your computer's firewall is enabled to block unauthorized access to your system.

Example: Using Windows Firewall or a third-party firewall software.

Tip: Regularly check that your firewall settings are enabled and configured correctly.

13.Disable Unnecessary Services and Ports:

Description: Disable services and ports that are not in use to reduce potential entry points for attackers.

Example: Turning off file and printer sharing on a computer that doesn't need it.

Tip: Regularly review and disable unused services and ports.

14. Secure Your Devices:

Description: Use biometric authentication (fingerprint or facial recognition) on smartphones and laptops for added security.

Example: Setting up fingerprint authentication on your smartphone.

Tip: Enable automatic locking and use strong passwords or biometrics to secure your devices.

15. Regularly Review App Permissions:

Description: Periodically check and update app permissions on your devices to ensure apps only have access to necessary information.

Example: Reviewing and adjusting permissions for social media apps to prevent them from accessing your location or contacts unnecessarily.

Tip: Uninstall apps that you no longer use.

16. Use Encrypted Communication:

Description: Use encrypted messaging apps like Signal or WhatsApp for secure communication.

Example: Using Signal to send messages that are end-to-end encrypted.

Tip: Ensure the apps you use for communication offer strong encryption.

17. Be Cautious with Downloads:

Description: Only download software from trusted sources to avoid malicious software.

Example: Downloading software directly from the official website rather than from third-party sites.

Tip: Avoid pirated content .

Certainly! Here's a more detailed essay on the topic of cybercrime in India and globally:

CHAPTER 16
CYBERCRIME: EMERGING CHALLENGES AND GLOBAL PERSPECTIVES

In recent years, cybercrime has emerged as a significant threat to individuals, businesses, and governments worldwide. With the rapid advancement of technology and the increasing interconnectedness of our digital world, cybercriminals have found new avenues to exploit vulnerabilities and perpetrate illicit activities. This essay explores the landscape of cybercrime, focusing on its prevalence in India and globally, the evolving nature of cyber threats, the impact on society, and strategies for prevention and mitigation.

In India, certain regions have emerged as hotspots for cybercrime. Rajasthan's Bharatpur and Uttar Pradesh's Mathura, along with Jharkhand's Jamtara and Haryana's Nuh, have gained notoriety for activities such as online fraud and hacking. These regions have seen a rise in cybercriminal activities due to various socio-economic factors, including access to technology, unemployment, and lack of awareness about cybersecurity measures.

Internationally, countries like Russia, Ukraine, China, the USA, Nigeria, Romania, and the UK are recognized as major centers for cybercrime. These nations are known for hosting cybercriminal networks that engage in sophisticated cyber operations, targeting individuals, businesses, and critical infrastructure.

The Evolving Nature of Cyber Threats

One of the most concerning aspects of cybercrime is its rapid evolution and adaptation. Cybercriminals are constantly innovating and refining their tactics to exploit new vulnerabilities and circumvent cybersecurity measures. For instance, the use of ransomware has proliferated in recent years, with cybercriminals encrypting data and demanding ransom payments in cryptocurrency, posing significant challenges to affected organizations and individuals.

Moreover, the anonymity afforded by the internet enables cybercriminals to operate across borders with impunity. This global aspect of cybercrime complicates law enforcement efforts and necessitates international cooperation and coordination to combat cyber threats effectively.

Impact on Society

The impact of cybercrime extends beyond financial losses and operational disruptions. It undermines trust in digital interactions, threatens individual privacy, and compromises the security of personal and sensitive information. Cybercrime can also have profound psychological effects on victims, leading to stress, anxiety, and distrust of online platforms.

Businesses face significant financial and reputational risks from cyber attacks. Data breaches can result in substantial financial losses, regulatory fines, and damage to brand reputation. For governments, cybercrime poses challenges to national security and economic stability, particularly when critical infrastructure and government agencies are targeted.

Strategies for Prevention and Mitigation

Addressing the complex challenges posed by cybercrime requires a multi-faceted approach involving technological innovation, policy development, public awareness, and international cooperation.

1. Technological Solutions:

- Deployment of advanced cybersecurity technologies such as AI-driven threat detection systems, machine learning algorithms, and behavioral analytics to identify and respond to cyber threats in real-time.

- Implementation of robust encryption protocols, firewalls, and intrusion detection systems to protect sensitive data and networks from unauthorized access.

2. Policy and Legislation:

- Strengthening of cybersecurity laws and regulations to deter cybercriminal activities and hold perpetrators accountable.

- Enhancement of international legal frameworks and cooperation agreements to facilitate cross-border investigations and extradition of cybercriminals.

3. Public Awareness and Education:

- Promotion of cybersecurity awareness campaigns targeting individuals, businesses, and educational institutions to educate them about cyber threats, safe online practices, and the importance of regularly updating security software.

- Integration of cybersecurity education into school curricula and professional training programs to build a cyber-aware workforce capable of recognizing and responding to cyber threats effectively.

4. Collaboration and Partnerships:

- Collaboration between government agencies, law enforcement, private sector organizations, academia, and international cybersecurity organizations to share threat intelligence, best practices, and resources.

- Establishment of public-private partnerships to develop innovative cybersecurity solutions and strengthen collective defense against cyber threats.

Conclusion

In conclusion, cybercrime represents a pervasive and evolving threat in today's digital age. From local hotspots in India to global cyber hubs, cybercriminals continue to exploit vulnerabilities and innovate their tactics to maximize their illicit gains. The impact of cybercrime on individuals, businesses, and governments underscores the urgent need for comprehensive strategies that encompass technological innovation, policy development, public awareness, and international cooperation.

By adopting a proactive and collaborative approach, stakeholders can mitigate the risks posed by cybercrime and build a resilient cybersecurity ecosystem. Empowering individuals with cybersecurity knowledge, enhancing technological defenses, and fostering global partnerships are essential steps towards creating a safer and more secure digital environment for all.

As we navigate the complexities of cyber threats, vigilance, education, and collective action will be key in safeguarding our digital future and preserving trust in online interactions.In the ongoing battle against cybercrime, several new technologies are emerging as powerful tools to enhance cybersecurity measures and combat evolving threats. These technologies leverage advanced capabilities such as artificial intelligence (AI), machine learning (ML), blockchain, and quantum computing to strengthen defenses and mitigate risks effectively. Here are some notable technologies and their applications in combating cybercrime:

1. Artificial Intelligence (AI) and Machine Learning (ML)

AI and ML technologies are revolutionizing cybersecurity by enabling proactive threat detection, real-time monitoring, and automated response capabilities. Key applications include:

Behavioral Analytics: AI-powered systems analyze user behavior and network traffic patterns to detect anomalies indicative of cyber attacks.

Predictive Analysis: ML algorithms can predict potential cyber threats based on historical data and patterns, allowing organizations to preemptively strengthen defenses.

Automated Incident Response: AI-driven systems automate responses to security incidents, reducing response times and minimizing the impact of cyber attacks.

2. Blockchain Technology

Blockchain technology, known for its decentralized and immutable nature, offers innovative solutions to enhance cybersecurity, particularly in areas such as:

Secure Transactions: Blockchain ensures secure and transparent transactions by creating tamper-proof records that are resistant to modification or hacking.

Identity Management: Decentralized identity platforms powered by blockchain enable secure authentication and verification processes, reducing the risk of identity theft and fraud.

Supply Chain Security: Blockchain enhances supply chain integrity by providing transparency and traceability, mitigating risks associated with counterfeit goods and tampering.

3. Quantum Computing

While still in its nascent stages, quantum computing holds promise for revolutionizing cybersecurity by exponentially increasing computing power. Potential applications include:

Encryption Breaking: Quantum computers could potentially break traditional encryption algorithms, prompting the development of quantum-resistant cryptography.

Secure Communications: Quantum key distribution (QKD) protocols enable the secure exchange of encryption keys, immune to interception or eavesdropping.

4. Threat Intelligence Platforms

Advanced threat intelligence platforms aggregate and analyze vast amounts of data from diverse sources to provide actionable insights into emerging cyber threats. Key features include:

Real-time Threat Detection: Continuous monitoring and analysis of global threat landscapes to identify new attack vectors and trends.

-Contextual Insights: Integration of threat intelligence with organizational data to prioritize threats based on their potential impact and relevance.

Collaborative Defense: Sharing threat intelligence across organizations and sectors to build collective defense mechanisms against cyber threats.

5. Internet of Things (IoT) Security Solutions

With the proliferation of IoT devices, securing these interconnected systems is critical to prevent cyber attacks. IoT security solutions focus on:

Device Authentication: Implementing robust authentication mechanisms to verify the identity of IoT devices and prevent unauthorized access.

Data Encryption: Encrypting data transmitted between IoT devices and networks to protect sensitive information from interception or tampering.

Firmware Updates: Regular updates and patches to IoT device firmware to address vulnerabilities and enhance security posture.

Conclusion

These new technologies represent a paradigm shift in cybersecurity, offering innovative approaches to combatting cybercrime in an increasingly interconnected world. By leveraging AI, ML, blockchain, quantum computing, and advanced threat intelligence, organizations can strengthen their defenses, detect threats proactively, and mitigate risks effectively. As cyber threats continue to evolve, continued research, development, and adoption of these technologies will be crucial in building a resilient cybersecurity framework to protect digital assets and ensure trust in our digital interactions.